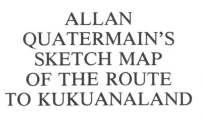

START OF THE
GREAT TREK TO
KING SOLOMON'S MINES

DURBAN ◯

esert

River

◯ Sitanda's
Kraal

ALLAN
QUATERMAIN'S
SKETCH MAP
OF THE ROUTE
TO KUKUANALAND

Characters:

Allan Quatermain, *the hunter, who writes the story*

Sir Henry Curtis,
an Englishman, looking for his lost brother

Captain John Good, *Sir Henry's friend, a naval captain*

Umbopa, or Ignosi,
the rightful king of the Kukuana people

Twala, *the king who murdered his brother*

Gagool, *the evil old woman*

Scragga, *cruel son of Twala*

Infadoos, *brother of Twala, uncle of Ignosi*

Foulata, *the native girl saved from sacrifice*

Neville, or George Curtis, *Sir Henry's lost brother*

José Silvestre,
the Portuguese who gave Allan Quatermain the map

bird Books Ltd Loughborough Leicestershire UK
Auburn Maine 04210 USA

LTD MCMLXXXII

KING SOLOMON'S MINES

H Rider Haggard

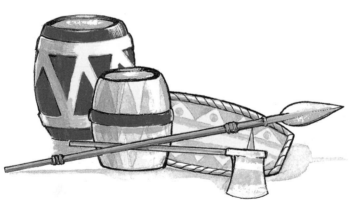

retold in simple language
by Joan Cameron

with illustrations by Frank Humphris

Ladybird Books

King Solomon's Mines

It is a curious thing that at my age — fifty-five last birthday — I should find myself writing a story. I wonder what sort of tale it will be, if I ever finish it?

My life has been an exciting one, travelling, hunting and mining in southern Africa. The story I am going to tell is a strange one, and it is time I made a start.

My name is Allan Quatermain, of Durban, Natal. Eighteen months ago I was aboard the steamship *Dunkeld*, returning home from Cape Town after an elephant hunt. Among my fellow passengers were two Englishmen.

The first was Sir Henry Curtis. One of the biggest men I have ever seen, he had yellow hair and a thick yellow beard. His companion, Captain John Good, was a naval officer. Neat and clean-shaven, he always wore an eyeglass in his right eye. I found later that he only took it out when he went to bed, together with his false teeth!

I was to come to know these two men very well. They were to share the greatest adventure of my life!

The first evening at sea, I joined the two men for dinner. When I gave Sir Henry my name, he leant forward eagerly.

"Mr Quatermain, I heard you were north of the Transvaal last year. Did you meet a man called Neville?"

"Oh, yes. He was with me for a fortnight before going on into the interior."

"Do you know where he was going?"

"I heard something," I answered, then hesitated.

Sir Henry and Captain Good looked at each other, then Sir Henry went on: "Mr Quatermain, I am going to ask for your help. Neville was my only brother, George."

"Oh!" I said, surprised.

"Some five years ago," Sir Henry explained, "we quarrelled, as brothers sometimes do. Just afterwards, my father died, without leaving a will. All his property came to me, as the elder son. My brother was left without a penny. Of course I would have provided for him, but our quarrel had been very bitter."

He sighed.

"Without telling me, he took the name of Neville and came to Africa in the wild hope of making a fortune. I have heard nothing since. Captain Good and I have come to look for him."

"I heard he was heading for Solomon's Mines," I told them.

"Solomon's Mines!" exclaimed both men. "Where are they?"

"I only know where they are said to be." I lit my pipe as I spoke. "I first heard the legend of King Solomon's Diamond Mines from an old hunter when I was a very young man. He told me that they lay somewhere beyond the Suliman Mountains, across the great desert. A race of Zulus lived in the country there, big, fine men who knew the secret of the 'bright stones.' I laughed at the story at the time, then forgot about it."

I looked gravely at the two men.

"However, twenty years later I was at a place called Sitanda's Kraal, and there I met a Portuguese, a man called José Silvestre. He was leaving to cross the desert, and he told me that when he came back, he would be the richest man in the world.

"A week later he crawled back into my camp, exhausted. I looked after him, but he was dying. Just before the end he gave me an ancient map, which was supposed to show the way to Solomon's Mines. It had been in his family for three hundred years. He had

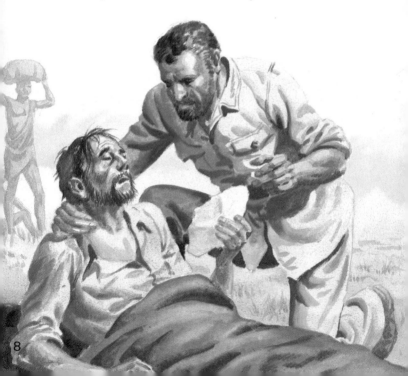

tried to follow it, but the desert had beaten him. I still have that map."

In my cabin, I took the tattered map from my bag, and the three of us looked at it together. With his finger, Sir Henry traced the route from the Kalukawe River across the desert, between the twin peaks of Sheba's Mountain and along Solomon's Road to the treasure cave.

"And you think my brother has gone there?"

"I'm certain of it," I said. "His hunter told me."

"Mr Quatermain," Sir Henry sat up, "I am going to look for him, with or without the treasure. Will you come with me?"

"We may not come out alive," I told him seriously. "But if you are prepared to take the chance, I will too."

Once the *Dunkeld* reached Durban, I took my new friends to my home, and from there we prepared for our great journey. We bought stores, and rifles and ammunition.

The day before we left, a strange man unexpectedly asked to see me. He was very tall, and light-skinned for a Zulu.

"My name is Umbopa," he said, lifting his knob-stick in salute. "I hear that you are taking white chiefs far into the North. Is it a true word?"

The reasons for our journey had been kept secret! I looked at him suspiciously.

"Why do you ask? What is it to you?" I demanded.

"It is this, O white man. I would travel with you."

"We know nothing of you," I said, puzzled at the dignity in his speech and manner. He seemed different from the ordinary Zulu.

"I am of the Zulu people, yet not of them," he told me. "I came from the North as a child, and have wandered for many years. Now I am tired, and would go North again."

I translated his words for Sir Henry and Captain Good. Sir Henry stood up beside him. Umbopa was a magnificent-looking man, wearing a leopard skin and a necklace of lion's claws.

"They make a fine pair, don't they?" Good said. "One as big as the other."

"I like your looks, Umbopa," Sir Henry spoke in English. "I will take you as my servant."

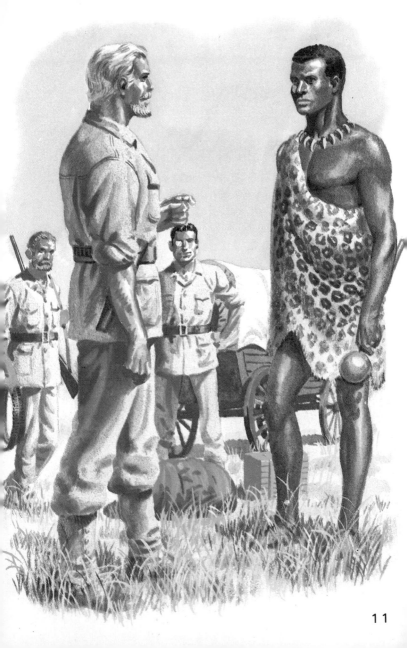

Umbopa evidently understood, for he answered in Zulu: "It is well."

It was settled. The first stage of our long and dangerous journey began the next morning.

We left Durban at the end of January. By the middle of May we had travelled more than a thousand miles. Umbopa was a cheerful fellow, and had the knack of keeping up our spirits when we grew weary.

At length we reached the edge of the desert, and stood looking out over the sand.

The sun was setting and the air was very clear. Far away we could see the faint blue outline of the Suliman Mountains.

"That is the wall around Solomon's Mines," I said, pointing to them.

"My brother should be there." Sir Henry's voice was quiet. "We will find him."

Umbopa had appeared behind us.

"Perhaps I too seek a brother over the mountains," he said. "There is a strange land yonder, a land of brave people, and a long white road."

I looked at him doubtfully. The man knew more than he would say.

"You need not fear me," he said, seeing my worry. "I will tell you all I know — if we cross the mountains. But Death sits upon them."

Sir Henry watched him walk away.

"That is an odd man," he said.

All next day we rested. As the moon rose, flooding the wild country with light, we set off across the desert. We were to travel by night to avoid the burning heat of day.

On we tramped, silently as shadows. Dawn came, and soon the sun was up, enveloping the desert in its fierce glow. We quickly sought shelter from the baking heat. Days and nights passed in the same way. Then came a moment when our precious water was gone.

"We must find water," I croaked.

Just in time, we found the water-hole marked on Silvestre's map, by following fresh springbok tracks in the sand. Joyfully filling both ourselves and our water bottles, we set off again.

The Suliman Mountains came closer. We left the desert behind, and began to climb the lava slopes of Sheba's left peak. Our water was

gone again, but we stumbled on a patch of wild melons. Poor fruit as they were, they saved our lives.

On we went, upwards, until we were climbing through snow. At last we stood, tired and hungry, on top of the huge mountain.

A glorious panorama unfolded itself to our gaze. Far below lay beautiful countryside. Here were dense forests, there a great river wound its silvery way across the plain.

Nearby, some antelope basked in the sun. Here at last was food! Out came our rifles, and we shot a fine buck. After we had eaten, we felt life come back to us.

"Look!" exclaimed Sir Henry suddenly. "There is Solomon's Road."

Good and I followed his pointing finger. There it was, not far below us. Walking down the hillside, we stepped on to the road. We looked at it in amazement, for it appeared to

be cut from solid rock. Walking was easy on its smooth surface, so we decided to follow it.

After several miles, we stopped by a stream to rest. All except Good, that is. Always a neat man, he wanted to be clean and tidy. First, he carefully brushed his trousers and coat, and took a bath in the stream. Then, clad only in his flannel shirt, he produced a pocket razor and began to shave his stubbly beard. I watched idly.

Suddenly, something flashed past his head. It was a spear!

Now a group of men appeared. They were tall and copper-coloured, and wore leopard skins and plumes of black feathers. One of them, a young man, had thrown the spear, for his hand was still raised. They all advanced towards us, led by an older, soldier-like warrior.

"Greetings!" I called to them in Zulu.

"Greetings," answered the old man, not in quite the same tongue, but in one so similar that Umbopa and I understood easily. "Who are you? Why are your faces white, and his like ours?"

He pointed at Umbopa, and I saw that his skin was indeed like theirs.

"We are strangers, come in peace," I replied.

"Strangers? Strangers to Kukuanaland must die! It is the kings's law."

"We are to be killed," I translated grimly for the others.

"Oh, no," groaned Good. And as was his way when perplexed, he put his hand to his false teeth. Dragging the top set down, he allowed it to fly back into his jaw with a snap. The next second, the dignified warriors uttered a yell of horror and bolted backwards!

"He moved his teeth!" whispered Sir Henry excitedly. "Take them out, Good."

Good obeyed, slipping the set into his sleeve. The men had crept forward again, curiosity overcoming fear.

"How is it, O strangers," asked the old man, "that his teeth move?"

Good promptly grinned, revealing empty gums. The audience gasped. Good swept his hand across his mouth, grinned again, and revealed two rows of lovely teeth.

"Ye must be spirits," faltered the old man. "How could a man have hair on only one side of his face, a transparent eye, beautiful white legs, and teeth which melt away and grow again? Pardon us, O my lords."

Good's appearance had saved us. Here was luck indeed and I jumped at it.

"We come from the stars!" I cried. "I will show you our strength. I will kill, with a noise."

Umbopa rose to the occasion, handing me my rifle and bowing low.

"Here is the magic tube, O lord," he said.

I had noticed a small antelope nearby. It was an easy shot. Bang! The antelope lay dead.

"Ye see I do not speak empty words."

"It is so!" gasped the old man.

"Listen, children of the stars," the old man went on. "I am Infadoos, son of Kafa, once king of the Kukuana people. This youth is Scragga, son of King Twala the Black, the Terrible."

"So!" said I. "Lead us to Twala. But play no tricks. If you do, the light of the transparent eye shall destroy you, and the vanishing teeth shall fix themselves in you — our magic tubes shall speak loudly. Beware!"

This magnificent speech impressed Infadoos. He bowed low and murmured the words "Koom! Koom!", which I later discovered was the Kukuana royal salute. At this, Scragga, the king's son, looked angry.

We set off again, along the great white road.

"Who made this road?" I asked Infadoos as we walked.

"None knows who or when," he replied. "The road was here when our race came from the North, like the breath of a storm, ten thousand moons ago. They could travel no further because of the mountains which ring the land. So says Gagool the Old, and smeller out of witches."

He waved an arm around him.

"Our people settled here and grew strong.

When King Twala calls up his regiments, their plumes cover the plain.''

''Tell me about Twala,'' I suggested.

''My elder brother, Imotu, became king when my father died.'' Infadoos looked sad. ''He was a good king, and had a small son called Ignosi. When Ignosi was three years old, a famine came on the land, and the people murmured. Gagool, the wise and terrible woman, said: 'Imotu is no king.' She brought Twala, who is also my brother, to the people and showed them the mark of the sacred snake around his waist. 'Behold your king,' she cried.''

Infadoos was silent for a moment, then went on: ''Twala killed Imotu, and made himself king.''

''What became of the boy Ignosi?'' asked Sir Henry.

''The queen took him, and ran away from our land. None have seen them since. They must be dead.''

Umbopa had been listening. The expression on his face was most strange.

While we talked we had reached the kraal where Infadoos lived.

Word had been sent on ahead, and now we had our first sight of a regiment of Kukuana warriors. Thousands of them waited for us. Each man wore a black plume on his head and a circlet of oxtails round his waist. As we passed, they raised their spears and gave the royal salute: ''Koom!''

We spent a comfortable night at the kraal. Next morning we continued along the great road to Loo, Twala's principal place. As we travelled we were overtaken by many warriors. They were hurrying to Loo to be present at the great annual review of troops,

Infadoos told us. More splendid troops I have never seen.

Loo came into view, an enormous place with a river running through it. Miles beyond, three huge mountains started out of the level plain.

"The great road ends there," Infadoos told us, pointing towards them. "The mountains are called the 'Three Witches.' They are full of caves. A great pit lies between them, watched over by the Silent Ones. The wise men of old time went there, to get whatever they came here for."

"What did they come for?" I asked eagerly. "Bright stones?"

"I cannot talk of it," Infadoos replied. "My lord must speak to Gagool the Old."

I turned to the others. "Solomon's Mines lie in those mountains!"

Umbopa broke in: "The diamonds are surely there."

"How do you know that?" I asked sharply.

He laughed. "I dreamed it in the night, white man!" Then he turned on his heel and walked away.

We arrived at Loo, and were taken to an open space in front of the king's huge hut. Before us thousands of warriors stood as still as statues. Twala strode out from his hut, a huge figure in a tiger skin. He was followed by Scragga, and what appeared to be a wizened, dried-up monkey, clad in a fur cloak. This was Gagool.

"Koom!" Out roared the royal salute. Dead silence followed, until one warrior dropped his shield.

"Kill him!" shouted Twala in tones of great rage.

To our horror, a grinning Scragga threw his spear. The unfortunate warrior lay dead. What kind of king was this?

Twala turned his cruel face to us. "Why should I not kill you too, men from the stars?" he demanded.

"This is why!" Swiftly, I raised my rifle and shot one of his own oxen. I could see he was impressed.

Suddenly, Gagool threw back her cloak, and revealed an aged, wrinkled face. She began to caper about.

"I smell blood!" she shrieked. "Ye white men come for diamonds. But who are ye, of the proud bearing?" She turned on Umbopa, her voice more piercing. "I know ye — take off your cloak . . ."

The effort seemed to be too much for her and she collapsed to the ground.

"Go in peace," Twala said uneasily. "Tomorrow I shall think of what Gagool has said."

Later, in the hut we had been given, I turned to Infadoos. "It seems to us that Twala is a cruel king."

"It is so, my lords," Infadoos bowed his head. "Tonight ye shall see the great witch-hunt. If Twala fears a man, or wants something of his, Gagool will 'smell' him out as a wizard and he will be killed. No man is safe. The people are weary of Twala's cruel ways."

"Why don't they cast him down?" asked Good.

"Scragga would then rule in his place. His heart is blacker than that of his father. If only Imotu or his son Ignosi had lived . . ."

"Ignosi is not dead!" Umbopa spoke directly to Infadoos. "See, I will show you, O my uncle."

He threw off his leopard skin. A great snake, tattooed in blue, wound its way round his middle. Infadoos stared, then fell to his knees.

"Koom! Koom!" he exclaimed. "It is my brother's son. It is the king!"

"Rise, my uncle." Umbopa put out his hand. "I am not yet king. But will ye help me overthrow this tyrant, ye and these brave white men?"

"We will!" we all cried. Infadoos promised to rally twenty thousand spears after that night's witch-hunt.

Umbopa, or Ignosi, as he should have been called, turned to us. "If ye help me, white men, what can I give ye? The bright stones — ye shall have them."

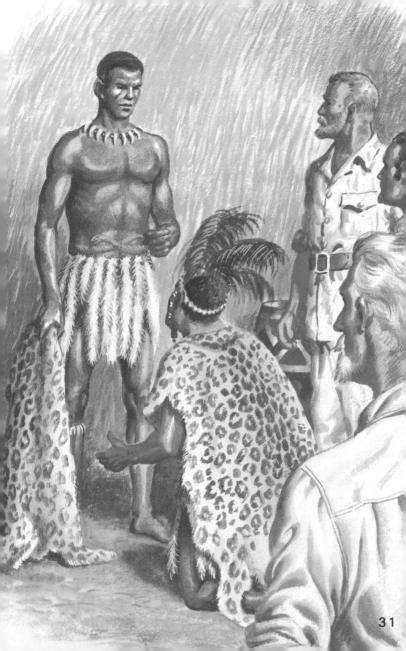

Sir Henry spoke up. "We will help you, diamonds or no diamonds, Umbopa. We came, as you know, to seek my brother. Has he been seen?"

"No white man has set foot in our land," Infadoos said. "I would have heard."

Sir Henry shook his head sadly.

"Poor fellow! So our journey has been for nothing."

That night we attended the terrible witch-hunt. Thousands of warriors were there, and the moon poured its light on a forest of spears. The wicked old Gagool began to dance around.

''I smell the evil-doer,'' she screeched, and pointed out the first to die. Her dance became quicker, and she pointed out man after man. They were all killed. At length she danced towards us.

"She's going to try her games on us!" cried Good in horror.

But it was Ignosi she touched. "He is full of evil. Kill him!"

I pointed my rifle straight at Twala.

"Stand back," I cried, "or Twala dies."

"Put away your magic tube." Twala was clearly afraid. "The dance has ended."

We returned to our hut, almost sick with relief. Infadoos arrived, accompanied by six stately chiefs. Ignosi showed them the tattoo of the sacred snake, and they examined it closely. At length the eldest spoke.

"The land cries out because of Twala's cruelties. But how do we know this man is our true king? The sacred snake is not enough. If we are to fight Twala, we need a sign."

"I think I have it," Good exclaimed, as I translated the speech. He produced an almanac. "I noticed that an eclipse of the moon is due for tomorrow night, to be seen in Africa. Tell them we will darken the moon!"

"Are you sure of the date?" Sir Henry asked.

"Oh, yes. I have kept a careful record."

"Very well." I turned to the chiefs and
addressed them in Zulu. "Tomorrow night we
will put out the moon. Deep darkness will
cover the earth as a sign that Ignosi is king!"

"It is well, my lords," said Infadoos. "Two
hours after sunset, the girls will dance. Twala
will choose the fairest, who will be given as a
sacrifice to the Silent Ones. Let my lords
darken the moon and save her life. Then the
people will believe indeed."

The next evening found us watching the
annual 'dance of girls.' Each girl was crowned

with flowers, and they made a beautiful sight in the moonlight. At length Twala pointed to a lovely young woman.

"Foulata is the fairest! She must die."

"Ay, must die," piped up Gagool.

Scragga lifted his spear in high glee. Unable to bear it, Good jumped in front of the terrified Foulata. "Stop!"

To my relief the shadow of the eclipse was just beginning to edge its way over the moon. I pointed upwards.

"Look!" I called. "We white men from the stars are putting out the moon. Let the girl go, Twala!"

A groan came from all around. The people scattered in panic as they saw the dark ring creep over the moon's surface. In fear or fury, Scragga threw himself at Sir Henry, brandishing his spear.

"The moon is dying!" he yelled.

There was a brief struggle, and at the end of it, Scragga was dead. The unholy shadow was swallowing up the moon. Even Twala had fled. We were alone, with Infadoos, Foulata, and six chiefs.

"Come," said Infadoos. "We have been given the sign. We must find a place to stand together."

As we left Loo, the moon went out utterly.

We established our warriors on a large hill, flat-topped and shaped like a horseshoe. There we would make our stand against the king's forces. When the sun was up, Ignosi spoke to his warriors.

"I am the true king. Who is with me?"

"Koom!" Raising their spears, they roared out the royal salute.

The first attack came, and a mass of struggling warriors swayed to and fro across the hillside. So fiercely did our regiments fight that Twala's men fell back. But we could see long lines of warriors advancing behind them. There had to be a plan for the coming battle, or our forces would lose. Ignosi had that plan.

''I will strike Twala this day!'' he cried, and explained what was to be done.

One regiment, led by Infadoos, would advance along the narrow valley between the two 'horns' of our horseshoe hill. Twala would send his forces to crush it. But the spot was narrow, and only a few could meet at one

time. Our other regiments would conceal themselves on the slopes above. They would fall on their enemies from either side, unawares, and trap them.

"If fortune goes with us, the day will be ours!" cried Ignosi.

The battle which followed is almost beyond my power to tell. I fought beside Infadoos and his men as Twala's warriors attacked along the floor of the valley. All I remember is the shaking of the ground under many feet, the dull roar of voices and a continuous flashing of spears around us.

A shout of dismay rose from our enemies, and I looked up. The place was alive with the plumes of charging warriors, both to the right and to the left. Twala's men were outflanked. In five minutes, the battle was decided. Taken by surprise, Twala's men broke, and fled.

The affair was not yet over. Ignosi had to deal with Twala, who had been captured.

"What is my fate, O king?" Twala asked in mocking tones.

"The same thou gave my father," answered Ignosi.

"I demand the right to die fighting!" Twala pointed angrily at Sir Henry. "He killed my son — I will fight him if he is not afraid!"

"I will fight," Sir Henry replied.

We watched fearfully as the two huge men rained blows on each other. The excitement grew intense, and I shut my eyes, unable to watch. At last the struggle was over, and Twala the Terrible was no more. Ignosi was king!

The battle over, Ignosi was greeted as king by the people of Kukuanaland. He told them there would be no more witch-hunts, and no man would again die without trial.

Later, we told him we were anxious to investigate the mystery of King Solomon's Mines.

"My people say the diamonds lie in a secret chamber inside the mountain," Ignosi told us. "There is but one who can show it to you — Gagool! I have saved her for this."

A few days later, we stood at the end of Solomon's Road. Our party consisted of our three selves, Infadoos, the maiden Foulata, who had made herself our servant, and the evil, unwilling Gagool. I shall never forget the awesome sight of the 'Three Witches,' and the great pit lying between them.

"Can you guess what that hole is?" I exclaimed. "Diamond diggings! I have seen them at Kimberley."

At the edge of the pit stood three huge statues — the 'Silent Ones' who guarded the secret entrance to King Solomon's Mines. Gagool cast a sly grin at us, and hobbled towards a narrow slit in the mountainside.

"I will show you the bright stones," she piped.

Infadoos stayed behind to set up camp. The rest of us followed Gagool.

We had travelled a long way into the heart of the mountain when at last Gagool stopped at a wall of solid rock. Then, as Gagool operated some secret mechanism, a great stone door rose up from the floor.

We passed inside to yet another passageway, which ended at a carved wooden door. Foulata would go no further.

Leaving her, we went into the chamber beyond. Sir Henry held his lamp high, to reveal a room full of stone chests. Some were filled with gold coins, many with diamonds. I fairly gasped. "We are the richest men in the world."

"Here are the bright stones ye love,"
Gagool flitted around. "Eat of them! Drink of
them!"

We paid no heed. We did not see her evil
look as she crept away.

"The stone falls!" Foulata suddenly cried
out. "Help! She has stabbed me."

We rushed down the passageway. Foulata
and Gagool were struggling together as the
stone door closed down. Foulata was badly

hurt, and could hold on no longer. With a shriek, Gagool twisted like a snake through the crack of the closing stone. Ah, but she was too late. Down came the stone on top of her. It was all done in four seconds. Foulata, too, lay dead at our feet.

"We're buried alive," Sir Henry said slowly.

Sir Henry was right. Only Gagool, who lay beneath it, knew the secret of the stone door. We tried to find the spring which operated it, but failed.

"It must work from outside," I said eventually. "Why else did Gagool risk crawling under the stone?"

I cannot describe the horrors of the day and night which followed. The lamp soon died and we were left in darkness, in a chamber full of useless treasure. Now we understood Gagool's mocking words of eating and drinking diamonds!

After an eternity, we noticed that the air remained fresh. Feverishly, we searched for a current of air, and found it, in a far away corner of the chamber. I struck one of our few remaining matches, to reveal a stone trap-door. We heaved it open. Another match showed stone steps leading downwards.

"I'll go first!" Sir Henry exclaimed, and Good quickly followed him. Before I left the treasure chamber, however, I filled my pockets full of diamonds.

A desperate journey followed. The steps led to a series of twisting tunnels, and we stumbled along them, exhausted. At last we saw a glimmer of daylight. The tunnel grew narrow, and rock gave way to earth. A squeeze, a struggle, and we were safely out, rolling over and over down a slope of soft wet soil.

Infadoos rushed up. ''Oh, my lords — you are back from the dead!''

We never did find the way back into the treasure chamber. At length we said farewell to our Kukuana friends, and left their lovely country.

And now I come to the strangest part of my

story. Infadoos had shown us another way out of Kukuanaland, through a mountain pass his hunters had discovered. Some miles into the desert lay a huge oasis. When we reached it, we found a white man there!

"Great powers!" cried Sir Henry. "It's my brother!"

And so it was. The man gave a shout and limped towards us. The brothers shook hands vigorously, their quarrel forgotten.

"I tried to cross the mountains, but hurt my leg," George Curtis explained. "I have been unable to move forwards or backwards since!"

Here, at this point, I shall end my story. We crossed the desert safely, although we had to help George Curtis all the way. Eventually we reached my home in Durban, and my friends returned to England.

But I shall see them again soon, for a letter has just arrived from Sir Henry. The diamonds I brought out of King Solomon's Mines in my pockets have been valued in London, and are of the finest water. We are all rich men. Sir Henry wants me to join him. I think I will take him at his word, and sail for England.

Stories . . . that have stood the test of time

Ladybird titles cover a wide range of subjects and reading ages.
Write for a free illustrated list from the publishers:
LADYBIRD BOOKS LTD Loughborough Leicestershire England
and USA – LADYBIRD BOOKS INC Auburn, Maine 04210